The Case of The Daring Two Face Bandit

ISBN: 978-621-434-059-0 (softcover)
978-621-434-060-6 (hardcover)

Printed in New York by:

OMNIBOOK CO.
99 Wall Street, Suite 118
New York, NY 10005
USA
+1 202-738-1322
www.omnibookcompany.com

First Edition

For e-book purchase: Kindle on Amazon, Barnes and Noble
Book purchase: Amazon.com, Barnes & Noble, and
www.omnibookcompany.com

Omnibook titles may be purchased in bulk for educational, business, fund-raising, or sales promotional use. For more information please e-mail
info@omnibookcompany.com

Design by: Gian Carlo Tan

The Case of The Daring Two Face Bandit

Swindler turned Preacher

Derrick Harding

CHAPTER 1

George is an educated man who lives a simple and sheltered life. Yet, he has reasons to break out of his conformity, when he is duped a thousand and five hundred dollars by an online hacker. Something must be done to put an end to his complacent ways. It isn't the first time and certainly, won't the last.

On September 9. 2008 his account is hacked. Yet, this long-lasting disarray doesn't break his iron clad will.

One Friday afternoon he goes to the supermarket. He fills a shopping cart with grocery as he sings along with the music being played for entertainment. He has a bouquet of red roses, that he is taking home to make his wife proud. He stands in line for nearly one hour. He makes light conversation with two ladies who sandwiches him. At last he pushes his cart toward the cashier. His cart is packed with goodies. The cashier smiles at George and gets to work. Her fingers tell the electronic tally machine the sum of his bill.

"Nearly one hundred dollars." George remarks in an undertone.

The cashier smiles and nods her head approvingly. So, with confidence he reaches in the left back pocket of his pants and pulls out his wallet. He retrieves his Bank of America debit-card and swipes it. But woops, he gets an error message. He tries twice. Suspicious eyes of shoppers decide his fate, whether he has, a bad account or not.

The cashier takes the card. With a frown on her brow, but she maintains a puzzled look, though she smiles at him. With instant aim she swipes once. The machine defies her intent. It gives that Friday afternoon, no pay check embarrassment message. Of course, George is dressed well and looks responsible. He can't be a fake, other curious shopping un-lookers think. He holds up his left hand and twiddles his married ring to confirm his status. But does he make sure that his check is lodged in the bank before he swipes his card? Different scenarios play out in his mind. Does the pay clerk get to forward the check to his direct deposit account? Does someone break into his account? And the list goes on in his head. Either way he is totally disappointed and embarrassed. Amidst the eyes of nearby shoppers, some sympathetic, others with raised eye brows. George walks out of the supermarket leaving the packed shopping cart behind. The cashier calls, "void". A supervisor comes to her aid and orders a worker to replace the goods on the shelf. This is only one of many incidents that George faces.

Another Friday afternoon on his way home from work, his car runs low on fuel. He pauses at the gas station where he always fills his car's gasoline tank. His gas needle borders on low. He is trying to fuel-up for the weekend. Who wants to get up out of one's bed on Saturday morning to join a line at the gas pump; worse yet, one needs to drive to Church on Sunday? Fortunately, he doesn't go inside to order gas like other customers. He just goes straight to the pump as he always does and swipes his card.

Sometime later he is told by a customer service representative at his local bank, that criminals cleverly steal your card information from the gas station pump.

Now, George has not just one, but two experiences to make him be cautious in using his card. However, he isn't the only one. It has become a pattern for criminals to target seniors and retirees, he is told.

The story is told of an old retired factory worker, a woman in her seventies. She has her savings slashed nearly in two because a swindler targets her and sells her a story that is compelling. "Her grandson is in jail and she must help him right away, he doesn't want to spend the night in that dirty cell."

Gorge has a similar story. Yet, he is no ordinary man. He is educated, he went to graduate school, he is the leader of the elder's-board in his church and he is a retired teacher. He was in the classroom for more than thirty years. But sadly, he hasn't gone to the "College of Hard Knocks or the university of Street-smart," although he has years of experience on his side. Yet, George is caught flat-footed.

It so happens, that you can fool some of the Georges most of the times, but you cannot fool all of them all the time, except this George. He who tells many con artists on the phone to take a hike. He who has his financial business well secured and can give advice to others; he who is giving advice to young people, comes under fire. A caller poses as his nephew and sells him a 'six for a nine' and he swallows it, 'hook, line and sinker.' He takes that bait and runs with it like a marline which swallows a hook and is in shock. Slowly and methodically it plays upon his emotions. "Uncle George, this is your nephew 'Phillip, he weeps believably, no doubt he is snorting streams from his nostrils.

"Can you help me?" His voice trembles.

"I have money and I will pay you back as soon as I get out. This man is handling my case." He tells him the name of the person and gives him the case number.

"He will call you."

The name Phillip traumatizes him for hours. You see, he is a good man, in his early forties. He grows up in a Christian environment and is serving the Lord. He doesn't make alcohol drinking, nor cigarette smoking as his habit, and he has no previous criminal record.

Yet, he is in jail because the alcohol level in his blood is higher than normal. This baffles George. He is now thinking about the young man's soul. Does he take on the habit of drinking? He asks himself. George can't think of him being in jail leaving his sweet twelve years old daughter on her own, unless he has strayed from his faith. Therefore, it is urgent to help Phillip as quickly as possible. He wires the seven hundred and fifty dollars via 'Western Union' the same day. However, this is his chance to make amends, ask questions and redeem himself, yet, he is slow to catch on.

The next day, the communication takes a different turn. The young lady who is involved in the accident that causes his arrest, was pregnant and she lost the baby. Hence, the bail bond is raised back to $1500.00, Phillip is charged with involuntary manslaughter and is remanded in jail to be transferred to another facility. George is asked to pay another seven hundred and fifty dollars. It is then that he becomes aware that they are swindling him. They refuse to allow him to talk directly to his nephew. So, they come under strong rebuke from George. The money which is to be sent back from the 'Treasury Department' as promised, comes to nothing. Two weeks later the real Phillip returns from his vacation from Jamaica to his home in Connecticut. He is told the wild story and he laughs because Uncle George allows himself to get con. Therefore, the crooks were only posing to be him.

So, there is a discussion now, among George's family at a gathering when they have a family celebration. The speculation suggests that there was a nephew involved indeed. This time it is Raphael the Romer, the two- face bandit, otherwise called Son-son, because he has no abiding city. He is the son of George's half -brother Roland. Roland marries to a young lady name Tena. Roland's mother is totally against the Union between them, but Roland loves Tena and they form an inseparable bond. Roland is a Farmer and carpenter in Jamaica. He raises the most beautiful livestock and cultivates ground provisions which he prefers to utilize for feeding his smaller brothers and sisters. He supplies them with milk and food stuff. While his dad sells to the community, he finds great pleasure in watching his impressionable siblings enjoy themselves. His nicest produce is given to his mother who prepares meals for them. He also builds pieces of furniture for the house as well as he does carpentry work on people's houses in the community.

However, after occupying himself in these capacities for some time, he decides to switch occupation. This time he decides to travel abroad, to the USA, to cut sugarcane in Bell Glades Florida, and to pick fruit in other parts of the United States. From all accounts he does very well for himself. One of his prize positions is a transistor radio which uses four big batteries. This is one of the first radios introduced into the community. It creates quite a stir. It is played from morning until night once Roland is at home. He plays music and dances with Tena his girlfriend. However, when it comes time for him to return to the states, he leaves the radio with his mother. She listens to "Back to The Bible Broadcast," daily

Roland and Tena eventually get married and are enjoying life together. It so happened, that he later migrates to England. Things don't work out well between them. She is possessive and tries to control the children. He can't talk to them without, incurring a dispute, whenever they misbehave. So, the children grow up wayward and out of control. As a result, they all go astray and don't rally around the parents.

Roland migrates back to the USA and carries Son-son with him which soon turns out to be a big failure. He drops out of college, and the military and becomes as Roland described him: "The No-good boy." One redeeming factor with Son-son is that he is a smart and handsome fellow. Every where he goes a young lady falls for his wild stories. He has several traffic tickets and somehow he gets them revoked. He has several children and he can't take care of them. For survival he has become quite a con artist. He will always be involved in some wiled schemes of financial dealings.

He borrows money from several women and can't repay them. When it comes to payment time, he changes his address and takes off. When you went to his house to find him, he is always out of town. Yet he will charm his way into the heart of other beautiful women. He plays tricks on two of his uncles and tries to use them. In the first incident he reports to his uncle George's house. He is wet with perspiration from his head to his feet. He tells him that he has stomach problem and he takes brook-lax tablets and it was upsetting his stomach. His uncle is not aware of his wild scheme of drug involvement. He sleeps on his couch for nearly two days. Then comes Sunday morning, his uncle makes breakfast and they eat. Then his uncle invites him to church. He provides him with a suite of clothes, for him to change his dirty suit. At church, he doesn't sit with him. Since his uncle George was an Elder and sits up near the front of the congregation, he chooses to sit near to the back.

After church they go back home. Son-son chooses not to travel with him, however, he shows up hours later. They eat and relax, but his uncle decides to go back to evening service. They drive to church and go back home later. Son-son decides that he has enough of his uncle's way of life, so he devises a plan to rob him, but his plan backfires. The house has burglar alarm. Since his uncle doesn't trust to leave him in his house, they both walk out Monday morning. His uncle goes to work, and he, to where he hangs out.

At 10.30 am, George gets a call from the police. His alarm goes off. The police say nothing seem to be missing but the alarm panel is broken. They give him a choice of locking up the house or will he choose to come to the house himself. He tells them to lock up the house. No one will attempt a second break in for the day.

When he comes home from work, two police men come to visit him. They grill him with questions but can't get the answer they need to put a theory together to conclude their investigation and build a case. Everything seems out of the ordinary, until one of the police men takes him aside and says "Come, now Sir, we are all men. Did you have a female guest for the weekend?"This was an inside job. Your back- glass door was left opened. Whoever you had for the weekend left your door opened because the person decided to enter your house in your absence."Though George is ticked off because of the question, since he is a married man and a Christian doesn't live that kind of life style, he sees wisdom in what the officer says. The person wasn't necessarily a female but a male. The alarm goes off and scares him away. The person tries to smash the alarm by digging the panel off the wall, but that also fails, so, he runs out of your house. "You need to check to see if you miss anything the officer says."

It is at that time that he figures out who is the inside bandit. One of the police gives him a contact card and tells him that if he learns anything more, to give him a call. George invites the alarm company to come and fix the alarm. Luckily a technician is working in the area, so, he goes there, and reinstall the alarm panel.

Then he starts to search his home and his belongings. All his drawers are intact. There are no missing papers. His pass port and bank book are right where he has left them. Then, he attempts to relax and watch television. Low and behold the antenna and the cable box are gone. He goes to the glass door and opens it. It isn't damaged. He looks outside in the back yard and sees a strange garbage bin. Therefore, he theorizes that it is Son-Son who has left the door opened and brought the garbage bin to put stolen things in it.

Three days later, George gets a call from him. His response is: "Come home son."

One afternoon when he comes home from work, Son-son appears. George hugs him, and he cries and snorts on his shoulder. George tells him that he loves him, and he forgives him and nothing he does will prevent him or God from loving him. Son-son tells him that it is the drugs he is taking that causes him to do those things. Suddenly, two police cars come up. The officers jump out with their guns in their hands. He can't move. He thinks that they are going to shoot him, so, he goes behind George and cries out: "Uncle, beg for me."

George pleads for him and tells the officers that he isn't pressing charges against him. However, the police suspect him in several robberies and fleecing old retired people out of their income. The police slaps cuffs on his wrist, reads him his rights and shoves him in the back of their transport. When the news brakes to Roland and circulates in his family, there is total confusion. A few family members are surprised about the arrest, some blame Ronald for the lack of training Son-son receives. However, most family members believe that it is Tena's doing. She didn't allow Roland to set discipline. The children have no boundaries, so, they do as they can get away with. According to Uncle Harry, this is likened to the time in Israel when there is no king to lead, and all men are prone to do as it please them to do. So, are his children. They are abusive, they go out and come in as they feel, and their dad can't speak to them. Their mother would side with the children. When they begin to get into trouble with the law, they blame Roland.

School is not a priority anymore. Their grades fall, and Roland is forced to step in. At least he can rescue Son-son his last child. He is a goodly child, smart and good looking. George migrates to the United States and takes the boy with him. He tells him of the great opportunities that await him in the land that can, make the poorest man rich, if he decides to work hard and follow the law. He paints a picture of the American Dream as the young boy listens with wonderment. He is sure that without the influence of his mother he can make something out of his life. His dad is proud of him, so, he begins to work with him. He emphasizes school and shows him the importance of getting an education in the land of opportunity. He merely does enough to get himself through high school. He could have done better but his past life haunts him.

He enrolls in college. However, his departure from the word of God to: "Train up a child in the way he should go, and when, he is old he shall not depart from it." back fires. And the good old- adage, "Bend a tree before it is grown" catches up with him. Since Sonson doesn't get early training in discipline; he lacks the fortitude to take on college work fulltime. Therefore, after a few semesters, he is numbered in the infamous statistical lists of dropouts.

CHAPTER 2

Roland can't understand. With all his encouragement Son-son won't budge. All he wants to do is to sit at home, in the days and watch television, invites friends to his father's home and idle the time. Son-son is carving a path for a disastrous future. Yet, over Roland's dead body this won't happen, so, he thinks. One day he has a man-man talk with him. Son-son agrees that he needs to discipline himself. Hence the place to find that discipline is to be in the military. Therefore, he chooses to go into the Marines. Hence, Roland has solved his big problem with his son. He is so proud of him, he breaks the news to Uncle Harry and uncle George. Good old Harry invites them to have drinks with him. Roland speaks of the boy's intelligence and smartness. "It won't be long before he becomes an officer of ranks. The sky is the limit for him." And the old seer Harry, reminds Roland that he must communicate with him often and encourage him to maintain good discipline. He must follow rules and obey commands. Three weeks pass but he doesn't answer any of his dad's letters. On the fourth week Roland comes home from work one Friday afternoon and finds him fast asleep.

This is bad news for Roland. His son whom he envisions to be building such illustrious carrier, is clad in his navy suit and he is snoring. He doesn't wake him. Instead he resorts to praying a simple prayer over his life. As all Christians would do. Lord protect my son, show him favor, redeem his life in Jesus name." He goes on to prepare dinner, but all this time he fears the worse. He calls Harry and George and tells them. They are also very surprised, but Harry being a wise older man never panic but encourages Roland to go easy, until he gets the full story out of him. He promises to visit the following day.

Harry visits them the next Sunday at 6:00 pm. Roland is preparing dinner.

"Hi Uncle, you are just in time for dinner." Roland thanks Harry for coming over to give thanks for the meal.

"I really appreciate your coming"

"Where is George?" Harry asked.

"He can't come today but I expect to see him tomorrow. I have not spoken to Son-son yet. Perhaps you can get him to open- up on why he is not home." So, what's the problem now son? You didn't stay in college and I was sure that you would have liked it in the Marine. You are bright and articulate, just the kind of person the Military is looking for. What do you have to say for yourself son?" Son-son looks at his dad. He looks at Harry. He begins to speak, but he stops. The boy gets angry. Then suddenly he says: "How come you guys decide to have a conference about my life without my knowledge?" Both Harry and Roland are very surprised. They promised not to tell George until they hear what his story is. They look at each other with wonderment. Then both men attempt to speak at the same time. "But Son" they attempt and Harry backs down and allows Roland to speak. "But Son," Roland continues. "Don't you think it is necessary that we know why you suddenly turn up at this moment? Your dad doesn't even know about this. At least somebody must take the responsibility. I assume that you come here because you don't want George to know. "But this is my home." So, what's the difference?" You used to live with uncle George. My brother loves you so much. "So!" You choose to come here so I must take the responsibility to know.

"Imagine I come, and you don't speak to me, you just assumed the worse. "Well sorry son," said Harry, butting in, we don't assume the worse, but we are concerned about you." "If you are concerned about me that much, you will just back off and give me a couple days to rest and sought out things in my mind for myself instead of conspiring to discuss my failure. Remember this is my life and I want to live it my way." "Of course, of course we understand son." Harry said. "But you say you want to decide your mind." Hay, will you stop treating me like a child or I am in court." At this point he gets up and goes to the bathroom and the men have time to confer.

Well Roland what do you think? I smell a rat. I can't imagine that he would respond like this. Something seriously must have happened." "Not necessarily," "How comes you say that?" "Because you never treated him with confidence and respect and spoke to him as a dad, before you decided to call me to speak to him." "Well, I should have spoken to him before, but do you think that gives him the right to speak to me like that." "That is something you must answer." Harry said, with his gurgling old chuckle. "It all depends on how you talk to each other in the past. If you had established an acceptable pattern of response to each other, then you ought to be surprised." But if this is the way you two spoke to each other there is nothing to be surprised about."

So, what are you saying now, are you blaming me for the way this boy chooses to speak to me? his dad?" I am not saying that, but remember the bible says in (PROVERBS 22:6 KJV.) Train up a child in the way he should go, and when he is old, he will not depart from it." I know it would come down to this. You have always blamed me for my children's behavior. Their mother had a strangled hold on their lives. I couldn't do anything to influence their upbringing." I tried my best. Did you? Grandpa and Grandma would quake in their guts to hear that boy speaks today. That boy's speech shows no respect for you, and that is something you will have to address. Probably this tree wasn't bend before it reached this stage."

How could I bend him?" "Stand up as a man, brace yourself up with the Hamilton's blood flowing through your vain and put your foot down. That wife of yours takes advantage because you haven't acquitted yourself as a man." "But If he did something that was wrong, and I spoke to him, Tena would 'fly down my throat.' "How comes you always harping on his behavior, are you better? She would say. Or she might have said: "Will you please leave the boy alone and allow him to grow up like other normal children. Everything you are ready to punish him, when you are no better." "Now, now, that is surely a discussion for another time." "You are seeing the fruit of those early seeds that were sown. So, what do you expect?" King James Version of the Bible says: For he that soweth to his flesh shall of the flesh reap corruption; but he that soweth to the Spirit shall of the Spirit reap life everlasting." Like in the natural so in the spiritual, if you sow corn you can't expect to reap peas."

Roland, I expect you to stand up like a man and lay down the rules of engagement, if he decides to continue living with you. You can't be if and but, you must see him as a man now and address him that way. He comes back from a world where he had to assume the role of a man. He is twenty years old. He has seen life in a different light. Now he comes home, he must be treated as such. The bathroom door opens, and the conversation stops immediately. Roland clears the table and Harry decide to take leave. "Ok Son-son, Roland let me know how things are going."

Roland puts the dishes in the sink and walks him to the gate. "Sorry brother, I am not directly blaming you for his behavior, and I am not blaming Tena. I am only asking you to be strong and be the man God called you to be. You can't see him as failure, not yet, not ever. He has great potential in him." Harry says.

Notwithstanding, his smartness, his father's mistrust of his mother, with all his uncle Harry's encouragement he doesn't want to go back to the military. Marine life is too restrictive and rigorous. Son-son decides that he doesn't want military training to do what he wants to do in life. He wants to become a businessman and he needs instant cash. He moves from job to job and can't settle down. His father talks him into going into the Police Force because of his super intelligence, but a few months from graduation he has a fight with his sub officer and beats him. Therefore, he is discharged.

IT is currently, that he starts doing drugs. He starts hanging out with a gang which became notorious for robbery and dope selling. His superior intelligence places him at the head of the gang. They target old people and retired citizens. They appear as painters, gardeners and handy men. They run errand for the sick, the aged and shut in. When these people go for doctor's appointment or when they leave their homes, they are well-aware, of the surroundings and can search the house for jewelry and cash. They very carefully replace the little details as they find them. Therefore, most times the one who is robbed doesn't find out until days or weeks after. By then the thief makes well his escape.

Son-son is steep in hard drugs and pot smoking.

It is during one of his bouts with drugs that he goes to George's house to rob him. He is unsuccessful. He leaves the back door to the house opens to give him access. The alarm and the arrival of the police scares him away. It is then he was picked up by the police. Although uncle George opens his arms and gives him a fatherly embrace and they cry and snorted together it was in vain. Uncle George couldn't save him. He had to be arrested.

Therefore, there is an identification process and he is identified as the same young man who goes to some of the senior's houses.

As a result, he is convicted in court and is sent to an Atlanta prison for 10 years. All his gang and family members hire a good criminal lawyer, the best that is available. He manages to get his sentence reduced to three years. This is the beginning of sweet sorrow for him.

Son-son wastes little time to get involved in a prison gang which calls themselves the Cardigan. They are known to be protective of new and vulnerable inmates, therefore, they have the approval of the prison guards. Yet, they are racketeers. They involve themselves in selling credit card, social security, phone numbers and identification numbers to scammers. They have the information stored electronically which, they had to keep as top secret between themselves and confederates on the outside. They choose to do this to states far away from the jail so that they can't be easily traced.

Several people in New York, California, Arizona plus Florida, had their accounts hacked. The gang always has money. However, the banks and financial institutions of these seniors work diligently to refund customers and set up security systems to protect their identity. George is one of those customers who is unfortunately scammed. But there is no immediate permanent solution to this issue.

"Protecting his personal and financial information have become a must, especially in a growing digital world. When He reviews the Best Identity Theft Protection services, the following identity theft statistics are categorized to help get a better feel for how and why this threat continues to be a problem for consumers, businesses, and governments worldwide. There are scores of identity protection agencies Three such agencies are ongoing, scanning for credit applications who submits your name, including retail credit cards, cell phone accounts, new mortgages and loans."

"Ongoing monitoring of your credit files is done at all three credit bureaus. These are Equifax, Experian and TransUnion. The three bureaus credit report and score updates are based on data from Email, text and phone alerts to promptly notify you of certain changes in your credit files recorded every business day at the credit bureaus.

He finds out that, Via the Internet they have ongoing surveillance of the Internet's financial black markets known to be frequented by identity thieves. Patented Internet scanning technology helps alert you if your Social Security number, registered credit cards and bank account numbers are available in non-secured locations. Online monitoring for changes to publicly available information which, if inaccurate or compromised by identity thieves, can cause you to be denied credit or employment.

Access to your personal publicly available information, conveniently organized into a single report. Then dedicated identity theft recovery unit guides you through the process of recovery should you become a victim.

One such company is 'Identity Guard' which provides unlimited toll-free personal customer service with access to credit education specialists Identity Guard of $1 million loss reimbursement insurance. If identity thieves steal your money, they will help you cover your losses." This is great news to George.

However, each financial institution has its own security system that protects their customers account. George's bank refunds the money withdrawn from his account. The security system works well for him. He can't make changes to his account over the phone. All changes must be made in person at a banking center. Regardless of the emergency he has on a weekend, he can't just call and get answers. All he gets is an apology for his inconvenience. He most visit, a banking center un Monday morning to make correction to his account or his files. Sometimes he is frustrated, and he curses and swears. He would like to ask the bank to stop the restrictions, but it will only result in more hackers getting to his account.

Mean-while, the Cardigans in their Texas enclosure continues their notorious practices. These men have people on the Black market whom they conspire with to defraud and disrupt the lives of older citizens and middle- class workers. Hundreds of people who get pay every two weeks has their finance disrupted. These crooks test your security by subtracting as little as one dollar and if you don't observe it, they delve into your account. This is one of the experiences George shares. He says his bank alerts him about a fraudulent activity on his checking account. He rushes to the banking center on Friday afternoon.

The bank is packed to capacity. He must wait nearly two hours to get to a customer representative. By then he is fuming. If he can get his hands around the necks of that crook, he would strangle him to death. Unknowingly, it is his own nephew Son-son who is masterminding the operation.

When he eventually gets to a customer rep, he has perspired, he opens his shirt by undoing the buttons leaving his bare undershirt. He begins talking so loudly that the security and the bank manager must quiet him. People in the line are so districted that some failed to hear when the buzzer went off to invite them for service.

However, George is made satisfied by what the bank does. He is told the hacker first tested the account by purchasing a $1,00 item from an unfamiliar website, then George makes a legitimately large purchase of $3.000 himself. Suddenly, the bank closes the account when they become suspicious of fraud. George now knows that he must be more observant of his account. He used to go to the gas station and swipes his debit card, the customer representative instructed him to desist that practice. Claes Bell, CFA (4, 2018) reported on four risky places to swipe your credit or debit card. He said: Debit cards and credit cards seemed like equally good payment options, but there was one critical difference: How unauthorized charges are handled.

If you spot fraudulent charges on your credit card bill, you could alert the issuer, decline the charges and relax. With a debit card, your money disappears instantly from your checking account and it can be tough — or impossible — to get it back.

Even clear-cut cases of fraud where victims are shielded from liability by consumer protection laws could cause significant hardship for debt card users. While fraud was always a possibility, being careful about where you use your debit card could help you keep your money out of trouble. Here's where you should be on your guard with your debit card. "And if you're looking for a safer place to park your hard-earned cash, an online savings account is a great option."

He offers four suggestions for protecting your card from scammers. Firstly, he says some outdoor ATM machines are the perfect place for thieves to skim the users' debit card says Chris McGoey, a Los Angeles -based security consultant. He explains that Skimming is a method of capturing a bank customer's card information by running it through a machine that reads the card's magnetic stripe. Those machines are often placed over the real card slots at ATMs and other card terminals.

He says you're better off using an ATM inside a retail outlet or other high-traffic, well-lit places.

Even the card terminals that card users must swipe to get into ATM vestibules are being used by criminals as a skimming site, says Julie Conroy, research director for the retail banking practice at Aite Group, a Boston-based financial services research firm. You can spot ATM skimmers by checking for ATM components that look beat-up or askew, she says.

Next Gas stations are favorite places for skimming. They are another danger zone for debit card users. The payment terminals at the pumps have many of the features card fraudsters love, Conroy says.

"In a gas station where you do have a whole bunch of pay-at-the-pump (transactions) and minimal supervision, it's pretty easy for a bad guy to put a skimming device on and put a little pinpoint camera there and compromise debit cards that way," Conroy says.

Thieves often use small cameras to capture footage of debit card users entering their personal identification numbers (PINs). Conroy says that even if a thief doesn't manage to get your PIN from such a device, he still may be able to duplicate the card's magnetic stripe and use it for "sign and swipe" Visa or MasterCard transactions. With the high potential for fraud in pay-at-the-pump debit transactions, it makes sense to use cash or credit cards when you fill up or pay inside at the counter.

Likewise, he says there is danger in on line purchases. Online purchases with Debit cards are a convenient way to buy products online, especially for those who don't like to use credit cards. Unfortunately, the web is one of the most dangerous places to make purchases, Conroy says.

"Online is the No. 1 place where consumers shouldn't use their debit cards," she says. "It's susceptible at so many points. The consumer could have malware on their computer, so it could be at their endpoint that the data get compromised. It could be a man-in-the-middle attack where somebody is eavesdropping on their communications via the wireless network. And then at the other end, that data goes into a database at the merchant. "As we've seen with some of the higher-profile breach events … that data is going to be vulnerable if (they're) not properly cared for," he says.

Aside from the potential for hacking at many different points in a transaction, a fundamental problem with using debit cards online, it is impossible to know who is handling your information.

Lastly Bars and Restaurants Would you be careful, for signs of fraud with that order?"

Restaurant servers don't ask that question, but they might as well be, considering it, it is standard practice for wait staff to take customers' debit cards behind closed doors.

"Any place where the card is out of hand" can increase the chances of fraud, McGoey says. "The guy comes to your table, takes your card and disappears for a while, so he or she has privacy," giving that person the opportunity to copy your card information.

Even restaurants without sit-down service can present a threat, says Conroy. Using debit cards to order delivery can be risky because cashiers tend to keep the usual customer payment information on file. That may make future orders more convenient, but small businesses rarely take the steps necessary to safeguard payment information, she says. Several authors concur with Clase Bell that these four places are dangerous to use tour debit and credit card. These include Denise Richardson 05.7. 2912, and Harvey Caldwell 03. 07. 2014

Now the FBI is getting closer to solving the puzzle of the notorious Cardigan support of hacking on the web and financial centers. Therefore, they decided to break out of prison and that is to turn Son-son's life around. He masterminds the jail break to the last minute and when they think that he will join them he turned down the opportunity. Then it is too late for one of them to take a knife to his throat. Immediately the break is noticeable when these twelve men who are always so visible are missing. Son-son is called in and tested in the most rigorous and brutal way. He is beaten mercilessly by two prison guards. Then they ask him to explain the breakage. The moment he gives a false answer he is given another savage beaten. To save himself from more punishment, he is forced to cooperate with the prison authorities. If he decides to testify against them he will have to be transferred to another facility. All eleven prisoners will be transported back to that Texas prison facility, so he must be taken, to another, outside the state's jurisdiction . Therefore, his whereabout will be unknown, but he is given three extra years for conspiring in the jail break.

The deal is signed by the governor and is made legitimate.

First, he takes the guards to the cell where the breaking originated. Each twelve prisoners take one plastic bag of the debris from the wall to his cell and uses it as a pillow. The break is planned by all members of the gang but only he decides to stay at the last minute. His date for release is coming up soon and he doesn't want to jeopardize his chances. The break takes place one early morning, just after the guards make their final check for the night. He is only able to give few of the Cardigan members whereabout; only the ones in Miami Florida, his hometown.

A man hunt is dispatched in and around the state of Texas because all of them couldn't cross the borders of Texas so quickly. Texas is bordered by the U.S. states of New Mexico, Arkansas, Oklahoma and Louisiana. Texas is in the southern region of the U.S. and is bordered on the east by the Gulf of Mexico, where it shares an international border with that country. Therefore, road blocks are mounted at all border crossings. Busses and train routes are intercepted, but the criminals didn't take public transport. They all ware masks to disguise themselves. They all decide to foot the journey, three miles from the crossing. This information is invaluable to the FBI. They act upon it and by the next afternoon they begin to reap success. Now they are scrambling to decide which out of state seclusion is appropriate to transfer Son-son. Finally, he is shipped off to a California prison to serve out his three years. God hears the prayer of the righteous. His dad had prayed for him.

King James Bible says: And we know that all things work together for good to them that love the Lord, to them who are the called according to his purpose. And in Christian Standard Bible. We know that all things work together for the good of those who love God, who are called according to his purpose. (Roman8:28) True enough, God always has a purpose for the lives of those who call upon Him out of a pure heart. "He isn't willing that any man should perish but that all should come to repentance." The song writer says: "The vilest offender who truly believes, that moment from Jesus a pardon receives." God is infallible, so are his words unchangeable.

There are three unchangeable laws of God. He is sovereign as his word. That means: He has supreme authority as his word. In Psalm 103, a magnificent hymn of praise. David praises God for His blessings and compassion as a loving and forgiving father for his children (vss. 1-18). He concludes with a universal call for praise (vss. 19-22), but he begins this call with a declaration of God's sovereignty (vs. 19) for it is God's sovereignty that gives Him the absolute freedom to do what He does in His blessings and showing compassion to frail and temporal humanity. (vss. 15-16).

Psalm 103:15-19 As for man, his days are like grass; As a flower of the field, so he flourishes. When the wind has passed over it, it is no more; And its place acknowledges it no longer. But the loving kindness of the LORD is from everlasting to everlasting on those who fear Him, And His righteousness to children's children, to those who keep His covenant, and who remember His precepts to do them. The LORD has established His throne in the heavens; And His sovereignty rules over all. God rules over that prison cell where Son-son vowed to finish his sentence uninterrupted. God looks around the corner and sees him down the road playing a crucial role in the prison and for His kingdom.

Next, God never violates His word. Once He utters a word it becomes a spiritual law. He is bound by his word. The scripture says in Isaiah: that His words will not return to Him void. They can't. He has commanded them using the words "shall not". It is like God is speaking to His words. He tells them that they "shall not" return to Him void. He then instructs the words as to what they should do.

And last, God is limited by His word. In Genesis God bequeath His sovereignty to man. Have dominion over all things. He doesn't need to, nor tries to take back His authority from man. Having made this discourse, God knows the plan he has for Son-son. "For I know the thoughts I think towards you, thoughts of peace and not of evil to give you a future and hope." says the Lord: (Jeremiah 29:11) His divine plan base on the simple prayer Roland prays over him has come to pass.

While he has a change of heart and seems to have drastically amended his ways, some of his fellow Cardigans are still at large. The law enforcement has caught up with five, but one vanishes in the Deepwater swamps in Texas. Efforts are being made to find him. So, six members of the gang are still unaccounted for. They keep the FBI very busy. As soon as they get a tip that one is residing at a certain location and the FBI moves in to capture him, he just vanishes like thin air. Several times the occupants of the residence are arrested for being accomplice.

The last such tip is that one is frequented at a house at the corner one twenty fourth drive and thirty second court. There is an instant lock down of all entrances from one ninety -nine street to the north, twelfth avenue to the west, one- eighty third to the south and seventh avenue to the east. Every house is searched within the blocks. This is very scary but each leader of the team of officers has a warranty that gives them the right to search but the bad guy doesn't turn up at the designated address.

However, three occupants of the house are arrested for possession of crack cocaine and ganga. The citizens around them are very relieved when the men come out of the house in cuffs. Often- times, the street corner will be lined around with cars and they play the loudest music especially on week- ends. Although George has his whole yard fence around with six feet douro metal fence and a large picket iron gate, he must open his gate to give the officers access to search his back yard.

Meanwhile the five Cardigans who are captured are placed in confinement at their separate prison cells. They are not allowed to communicate or assemble. They are not let out for any reason as the man hunt continues for the rest of them. An incentive of $1000 is offered as reward for information leading to the capture and arrest of each prisoner.

It so happened at that time, that Son-son has a life changing encounter with the Lord. The Chaplin who leads devotion one morning tells a story to the audience in jail. The story says there was a middle eastern farmer, a shepherd, who had one hundred sheep. He knew them by name. He called them out of the fold to join him on a mountain where they would feed for the day. Later in the evening he noticed that the skies suddenly became dark. Low lying cumulous clouds hung very low and that was the threat of a very bad thunder storm. The wise shepherd called all the sheep and hurried down the mountain to the sheep fold. On reaching, he counted them as he called their names and they walked inside. He counted them from one to ninety- nine, but one was missing. He called him by name. White-white; he got no answer. He called out again White-white his favorite sheep didn't answer.

: (John 3:16. 17) says: For God so loved the world that he gave his one and only Son, that whoever believes in him shall not perish but have eternal life. For God did not send his Son into the world to condemn the world, but to save the world through him." From this text, he spoke on three points

1. God so loved the world.
2. He gave His only son
3. He did not come to condemn the world.

He began by saying: None of God's kindness in any way means He approves of the conduct of man's sin. Rather it is a revelation of His nature that, despite men's wickedness, He has compassion toward them. It is His earnest desires that man will be happy, and He could not achieve this extraordinary process except sending His son the Lord Jesus to die on the cross. He points out that the shepherd's dying is symbolic of how Jesus died. just as the shepherd's life is taken, so, that the sheep can be saved so each of you represent this sheep. Every man in the world should have died but Jesus, God Son took their place. He so loves the world that much.

Then He gives- His only Son that whosoever believes in Him should not perish but have everlasting life. If a man has several sons, he may be very reluctant to give up one to die. Yet, God has one son and He sacrifices Him for your sins and mine. If you believe in Him, you will not die but have everlasting life.

Last, He doesn't come to condemn the world but that the world through Him might be saved. The law condemns you, finds you guilty and incarcerate you. You are liable for the crime you committed. Now you are serving time behind bars. Yet, regardless of what you have done, God doesn't condemn you. That is why He comes. In the eyes of the law you are condemned but in the eyes of Jesus you are loved eternally. The bible says: For if your heart condemns you, God is greater than your heart, and knows all things.

He knows what is going on in your heart right now. You want to apologize to the people you wrong, you just want to put the past behind you and start a fresh. You want to live a new life. The men listened with rapt attention. A few get up and walk out, but Son-son listens and twitch uneasily. At the end, the Chaplin prays the Sinners prayer with the group. Everybody walks out except Son-son and another inmate.

Son-son doesn't give the other inmate a chance to speak. He just pours out his story how he fails to finish college, he fails to graduate from the Marine and the Police Force. He tells of his turning to drugs, breaks into his uncle's house and spearheads the gang in prison which defrauds hundreds of people. Then, he asks if God can forgive him for all those bad things.

The Chaplin looks at him and quots (1st John 1:8-9) If we claim to be without sin, we deceive ourselves and the truth is not in us. If we confess our sins, he is faithful and just and will forgive us our sins and purify us from all unrighteousness. Then he emphasizes "All sins or unrighteousness." He hears the other inmate's issues. They are just as similar, to Son-son's. He also wanders if God can save him. The Chaplin prays over their lives and says good bye.

Within a few days, Son-son is called into the Parole's office to start preparation for his parole. He learns that California has a state-wide mandate for Parolee. The mantra is: "Today's Offender is tomorrow's neighbor." The Step-By-Step Process is:

- Offender's risk to going back (criminogenic), the things that can cause him to revert, are assessed.
- Offender meets with their correctional counselor and is placed in appropriate programs and/or education, based on rehabilitative needs.
- Offender may be placed in various educational programs, including Academic and Career Technical Education.
- Offender may receive Cognitive Behavioral Treatment programs, including: Substance Use Disorder Treatment, Anger Management, Criminal Thinking and Family Relationships.
- Specialized programming is available for eligible offenders receiving long-term sentences.
- Offender can apply for a California Identification card.
- Offender may also enroll in community-based programs designed to help them successfully reenter the community from prison.
- Parole Agent enrolls the parolee in programs specific to their rehabilitative needs.
- Needs-based programs can include:
- Connection with Housing Resources, Life Skills, and Family Relationships
- Academic and/or Career Technical Education,
- Employment Assistance
- Parolee successfully rejoins society.

As a result, Son-son begins his journey by going to classes to study for the GED since he fails do well at High school. After three weeks Son-son discovers that some of the work is indeed very easy. Therefore, in one year he wraps up the GED program and moves on to the bachelors' in Architecture, and construction management. The course is a four years degree program, but he has only two and a half years in jail. So, he decides that He will complete his studies when he is released. In accordance with their Needs-based programs housing is promised to him when he gets out.

Meanwhile, Son-son begins a simple bible reading group. They read the bible every night just before lights out and talks about it during lights out. This is made easy because all five men occupy cell beside each other. One night one of the jailors hear the loud reading and went to investigate. He pulls out his New Testament and begins reading with them. He goes and spread the word. Soon two of his collages came and joined them. This simple gathering starts a sustaining revolution in the jail. The men begin holding public gatherings and discussion about their faith and the word of God. The Devil is present to disrupt the proceedings. A hate group that calls themselves: "The true Blood," who wears tattoos over their entire upper body symbolize the group. They swear that they don't deal in violence. Yet, inmates report that they are saved from a beating that they were about to perform. Therefore, the other inmates decide to combat their hostility by moving about together in groups of five. Son-son has three more months before his parole. He is invited to the hearing.

Notwithstanding, he gets permission to make a presentation before his release. To his pleasure the Chaplin and his friend will be present. It is obvious that he is not liked by some sectors of the inmates. Sections of the jail must be put under lock down. Hate messages are written on the bath room wall and mirror. He discloses this when he is called in for his parole hearing.

According to the connection with Housing Resources and skill training, he is promised free housing until he has completed his studies. He has one and a half years to complete it and graduate. Therefore, he is also promised reduced tuition fee and free books. He is set to be released on the day after the speech. This is kept confidential. He will be able to return to society.

At the commencement of his presentation he rehearses the story that the Chaplin tells on the morning he is converted. Then he asks a potent question: If a man dies shall he live again? All the days of my appointed time will I wait until my change comes the word of God says. (Job14:14) Every man must wait until his turn comes. If he takes matters in his own hand that will be suicidal. Because Paul labors and waits his turn he can write: "I have fought a good fight, I have finished my course. I have kept the faith; henceforth there is laid up for me a crown of righteousness, which the Lord the righteous judge shall give me at that day, and not to me only but unto all them also that love His appearing." Son-son says Stephen doesn't have that chance when he is mortared. He says Lord lay mot this sin to their charge. Similarly, Jesus only says: "Father forgive them for they know not what they do" But normally we must wait until our time comes. Some of us our time will come in season of prosperity, spiritual renewal or in adversity.

So, let us review the story of the good shepherd. Chaplin says that he represents Jesus. He has one hundred sheep. Each of you represents one of those sheep. He usually feeds them on a mountain side. This mountain over- looked the town. It happened on a day that he hurriedly returns the sheep to the fold because heavy showers of rain threaten. He usually counts off the sheep when he returns them. On that day, his favorite, White-white is missing even after recounting them. With concern on his mind, he locks the fold and hurries back to the mountain path to find him. Just as Jesus leaves the ninety-nine to look for me and you. As He finds him and lovingly clasped him in his bosom, a flash of lightening comes and structed him down. He is found with White-white folded under him protected, but the shepherd is dead.

This is synonymous of what Jesus does on the cross. He takes our punishment. He dies to make us live. God provides death and life, hell and heaven. One of the old patriots says to Israel. "See, I set before you today life and prosperity, death and destruction. For I command you today to love the Lord your God, to walk in obedience to him, and to keep his commands, decrees and laws; then you will live and increase, and the Lord your God will bless you in the land you are entering to possess.

But if your heart turns away and you aren't obedient, and if you are drawn away to bow down to other gods and worship them, I declare to you this day that you will certainly be destroyed. You won't live long in the land you are crossing the Jordan to enter and possess.

This day I call the heavens and the earth as witnesses against you that I have set before your life and death, blessings and cursing. Now choose life, so that you and your children may live and that you may love the Lord your God, listen to his voice, and hold fast to him. For the Lord is your life, and he will give you many years in the land he swore to give to your fathers, Abraham, Isaac and Jacob. He says, if it seems evil unto you to serve the Lord, choose you this day whom you will serve. He completed his quote by saying as for me and my house we will serve the Lord."

Then he tells if a man dies he must live in one of two places hell or heaven. So, he says, my question to you is: If you die will you live again and where will you live? This isn't an issue to put off because it is appointed unto man once to die but after death, then comes the judgment. If you die it is too late to make a choice. For some people it is too late even while they are still alive. They may be terminally ill and loose consciousness or their ability to understand. None of us knows how the end of our life will play out. Some of us won't live to get out into the society and others may not live once we get out. Society is harsh against ex-criminals. Once a criminal always a criminal for some people. Our only hope for survival is in Jesus Christ. No money, family ties, gang nor friendship can rescue us. The law might forgive us because we serve our sentence, but john public is still waiting to get us. Don't make the mistake and think that we will have any sympathy from the public. Give your heart to Jesus: Paul says for me to live is Christ, for me to die is gain. When we were in our element, we always have a game plan. Those game plans didn't work for long. They were not full-proof, or we would not find ourselves in here in the first place. Now you can invest your life in a full proof game plan by giving your life to Jesus, he says. He hands over to the Chaplin.

He sings a song and prays for the inmates. On this day almost all the inmates present makes decisions to follow Christ.

The next morning it is noticeable that Son-son is missing. He never shows up at breakfast.

Son-son boards a greyhound bus and heads for Florida. He will live in Miami and attend Miami Dade College. He has a busy schedule. He has an interview for his job at an Architectural firm where he will work as an apprentice. The interview is rather informal. He just needs to sign some papers and do finger print. He also takes an oath to obey the rules of the firm, which everybody does at hiring. Next, he will go to the college for registration, chooses his classes and collects his books.

He is promptly visited by his Parole officer. One of his duties is to take him to a near- by bank of his choice to open a compulsory savings account. He gives him forty dollars. Twenty dollars are to open the account which he sits with him and gets it done.

He also visits his home to see what his living arrangements are like. It is comfortable boarding facility with a retired parole officer. He pays three hundred dollars per two weeks. He must wash his own clothes and make his own bed. His pay check is sent to his bank account, from which he can only draw certain amount, except he gets permission from the bank. He lives a simple life, goes to church every Sunday and is never late for classes. He has special preference to do after class studies. He finds two guys that he is comfortable with for study group. The two fellows decide that there shouldn't be discussion about their personal lives. To which Son-son does doesn't agree. Therefore. he is up front and declares who he is, an ex-con who is living for the Lord. He doesn't feel ashamed of the gospel of Christ for it is the power of God unto salvation.

It so happens that all three are ex- convicts who are Christians. This makes life very comfortable for them. Each day before they start their study, they share the scripture. Each person takes a different day to share. However, they have noticed a strange occurrence each day after class when they meet to read and study the word. There is always a strange man sitting before them on a far away table. He is always reading his newspaper. Occasionally, he may read a novel. He never looks at them. However, his intentions are made clear one day when a black SUV drives up suddenly. He jumps up and shouts at us "Get down." He pushes his hand behind his back and the truck speeds away.

It is then he reveals himself to us, that he is Craig Lore of the FBI. He said one of the inmates who escapes from the prison in Texas finds out about your coming to college here in Miami, so he comes looking for you. He will be back, but we will be waiting for him. He won't get to hurt you. In the meantime, you can't go back to your address. Your Landlord can protect himself, but we don't want to take any chance with you. You have been nothing but exemplary. We want to get this guy. He won't get you. Don't call home. Let them call you. I will inform them of what they need to hear. His car was parked in the back- parking lot. How about my friends. You guys need to come with us. We left through the back entrance. The next day we didn't sit outside. We remained in the class room.

It is then we heard gunshots and cars racing around the campus. We knew just what it is. A little later we hear the fire rescue truck and sea the rescuers lifting a dead man into the truck. Craig comes and tells us that we ccan go home. He cautions us to be careful. The dead inmate, Samson, is the last of the bunch of those who escape. So, Son-son can go on with his life.

However, when you have a calling on your life, you can't but pursue that goal. Son-son has a calling on his life. English Standard Version of the bible says, . preach the word; be ready in season and out of season; reprove, rebuke, and exhort, with complete patience and teaching. Therefore, he is committed to his calling. At the church he attends he is involved in the Men's ministry. God uses him mightily to speak to the men. Therefore, he finds his purpose. He found the "Men in Action Program." They move from church to church to evangelize men. Men in Action decides to hold a three-night crusade. They work tirelessly to prepare. The crusade will take place on that Thanks Giving weekend, in one of the largest Churches. In preparing, they walk around the communities and hands out fliers. The opening night see the church filled.

Son-son will preach the first and the last nights, Friday and Sunday nights. Friday night he takes his text from St. John's Gospel, "I am the good shepherd, the good shepherd gave his life for the sheep." He illustrates his text by using the story with which he has now become familiar. He first hears it from a Chaplin in California jail. He tells the story of White-white. How the good shepherd dies and protected him. He tells the audience that he has a choice to wait until the next day but because he loves him so much, he is committed to go and find him that afternoon, through very heavy rain. He goes out calling, "White-white," and he hears his faint bleating.

His graphic illustration shows how the Shepherd curls up to protect the young sheep, his friend. He tells them that the sheep knows his master's voice. That's why when he calls White-white he answers. Jesus knows our voice. He hears us when we call. The sheep doesn't know the voice of strangers. Jesus is the Good Shepherd who gives His life for us. He redeems lost sheep. We are lost sheep the scripture says: "All we like sheep have gone astray but the Lord has laid the iniquity or sins upon Him." Right now, He is calling you. The song says: "Jesus is tenderly calling today, calling to day; calling to day. Jesus is calling is tenderly calling you home." The scripture says: "Behold He stands at the door and knocks, if any man hears His voice and opens the door, He will enter in and have fellowship with him." But first you must be in fellowship with Him. We get to be in fellowship with Jesus when we accept Him as Savior and Lord. We accept Him as our Savior when we invite Him to live in our heart. We do this by praying a simple prayer. If you pray this prater after me, you are doing just that. "Dear Lord, I am a sinner. I need you to come into my heart and save me from my sins. Wash me in your blood and create in me a clean heart. Give me grace to serve you and follow you amen."

Those who pray this are invited to write their names and phone numbers, given some literature to read and are advised to go to a church of their choice. On Saturday morning each person whose name is written is called and is prayed for and invited to the night's service. At the night service another brother preached. He took his text from (John 3:16-17 16) For God so loved the world that he gave his one and only Son, that whoever believes in him shall not perish but have eternal life. For God did not send his Son into the world to condemn the world, but to save the world through him.

He spoke on three thoughts from the text 1. God so loved the world. 2. He gave His only son. 3. Whoso ever believes in Him, shall live forever, that is have everlasting life. He concluded that God is so loving and hind, that He sent His Son not to condemn world but to redeem it. A similar procedure followed as the night before, but special prayer was given on behalf of those who were coming back for the second night.

Sunday morning Son-son and many visitors gathered for worship at his church. They welcomed those who accepted the Lord as their Savior. On Sunday night, Son-son was to preach, the closing message. He took his text from Job 14:14 He introduces his text "If a man dies shall he live again." Suddenly pandemonium broke out. A lone gun man came running from the back of the church shouting: "I will see if when you die you will live again." This was followed by an out burst of gun shots. A couple of the men jumped on the gun man and overpowered him. They pinned him to the floor and heard him shouting: "This man is an ex- convict. He is a jail bird. You can't trust him." After he had shot him. In the mean -time, someone called 911 and the police arrive, and the men handed over the gunman to them. Suddenly they remembered the preacher who fell behind the pulpit. He was suffering from gun shot wounds. The three men rushed to his rescue, while the congregation continued to shout Jesus, Jesus.

Some were sprawled on the floor between the pews. Others jumped over the benches trying to make their escape. The paramedics came and took care of Son-son and rushed him to the emergency room. At last things calm down. The police investigative squad moved in and cleared the building. They picked up spent shells and discovered that only Son-son was shot. The audience scattered outside. Some were dazed. Paramedics had to treat some for shock. One of the men invited the splintered audience to gather, hold hands, prayed and all left the scene.

Dillion Reid, the suspect in the shooting that wounded one person at a historic Denominational church, on Sunday night, was arrested at the scene of the crime and booked at the Miami Place Police station to appear before judge Stanley Roper on Monday. The men who overpowered him were praised and honored for their heroic job. Meanwhile, the victim is identified as twenty -five- year old Ex-convict turned preacher, Son-son Hamilton. He was critically wounded and taken to Jackson Fair Prospect hospital where he is battling for his life, but his condition is stable. This incident has left the community mourning, one report said.

It is reported that the shooting took place about 9 p.m. Eastern time Sunday night at the Emanuel Apostolic Baptist Non-denominational church.

One man was critically wounded. The suspect is in custody.

Miami Place Police Chief said the gunman entered just when the preacher introduced the preacher introduced his text, shouting hate slogans. "This man is an ex- convict. He is a jail bird. You can't trust him." After he shot him. He will investigate the shooting as a hate crime. The Justice Department's Civil Rights Division, the FBI and the U.S. attorney's office for the District of Miami Place have also opened hate crime investigations.

All the churches in the community have organized prayer vigil. Some church declared fasting and prayer.

The journalist covering the case went to the hospital to glean whatever news he could get. The doctor in charge of his case gave a brief interview. His case was serious, but he was favored to pull off a spectacular miracle. He got two shots, one grazed his left shoulder but the other penetrated his lungs. He was still heavily sedated. This affects his breathing, but he has passed the worse. He is supposed to make a full recovery. His story went viral "Ex-con shot in the pulpit." Hate crime is suspected. The story was broadcast by several television stations which were lined up for interviews.

This incident served as motivation for "Men in Action" those who accepted the Lord as their personal savior became militant in witnessing. Several new members committed themselves to the group. As soon as Son-son was conscious he inquired about his support group. He was given a full report that made him pleased. Then he was bombarded with telephone calls from radio and television stations. First, they wanted to know if he had any idea about who would want to kill him. As far as he knew he was a target for many haters. He said it is alright for them to hate him because that is what sinners do. He told about his pass and passage in jail that led to his conversion. He told them that he was not proud of his pass, but Jesus forgave him. If any man be in Christ he is a new creature, old things are passed away and all things become new. He wished that he could find every person whom he hurt but Jesus does not expect him to do that. So, He bundles all those sins and cast them in the sea of forgetfulness.

One journalist asked about his conversion and he described the story of the Good Shepherd that led to his accepting the Lord. He told of the incident when the inmate searched and found him, and he was shot. They asked about his future and he explained the study program he was pursuing but ultimately, he wanted to preach the gospel and he became emotional. He said: "For I am not ashamed of the gospel of Christ for it is the power of God unto salvation. He said that he forgave the man who shot him. When your life is controlled by Satan you are prone to do anything. He then prayed for his gang friends in jail, all the people he had hurt, and he asked that they forgive him. His interview went viral. On the first day it had five thousand hits, and the days after the numbers grew enormously.

Son-son was released from hospital riding in a wheel chair and utilizing a small oxygen device. It's a portable oxygen concentrator that can be worn effortlessly by active users without any worry of running out of oxygen, because it replenishes itself. He was excused from classes for six weeks to recuperate. Being out of classes for this time, meant that he had to catch up to meet the requirements to graduate. His job at the firm was secured. His being absent didn't incur any penalty.

Meanwhile, Son-son was bombarded with letters and email as well as face book messages. Chief of them were messages from ex-convicts reporting on how they turned around their lives. When they heard what had happened to him they surrendered their life to Christ. One of his offenders was one from Texas jail who had tried to kill him. He begged for his forgiveness. One correspondence came from the Citizens. "For, the Elderly in Action" which said: Congratulation on your recovery. We are very proud that you have turned around your life. Since you are only one who steal our money we forgive you.

Meanwhile Son-son resumed classes. He failed his first test by one point because of absence from classes and his lack of concentration because of the sickness. With his friends working with him he was soon brought up to speed, he was relieved from the wheel chair, but he had to accommodate himself with a walker. IT was sought of awkward at first but soon he found it easier. It is said that "Necessity is the mother of invention, then laziness is the father." He was not lazy, but he had to quickly adjust to using the walker and carry his book bag. He also adjusts to his class work by doing a series of male up work. He also resumed going to church, but he didn't start taking active role. Surprisingly, one day he received a letter from one of the offenders from Texas jail who had tried to kill him. He begged for his forgiveness. Similarly, he got correspondence from the group which had broken out of jail that they had changed their lifestyle. When they heard what he had done with his life they all embarked on a course of study to get their GRE. One confessed that he hopes to be a preacher one day. He asked him to send him a study bible. Meanwhile Roland was full of praise for him and George and uncle

Harry were confident that their nephew had made their mother and father proud.

I must confess that this story is partially true. I am Uncle George. My real name is Simon Indra Marshal, Sim for short. I was the one who was duped $1500.00. I am 72 years old and retired. Criminals target older folks like me with their wild but believable stories. Like the one which was told to me about my nephew in Jail. You know how older folks feel about their grandchildren and nephews. The following are pertinent suggestions download from (New KCK program to help senior citizens protect themselves from scams) (41 KSBA Kansa City) by:

Sarah Plake
7:05 PM, Mar 2, 2018
11:19 AM, Mar 4, 2018

Never give out social security numbers or other personal information to someone who calls

A government agency will not contact you for personal or financial information over the phone

If someone suspicious calls asking for money, or you think they might be pretending to be someone close to you, always question it. A common scam is someone telling you that you've won money, but you have to send them money first. Always contact police to report any scams. "The more people know, the more they can help themselves, be protected against all these scams that are going on.

www.ingramcontent.com/pod-product-compliance
Ingram Content Group UK Ltd.
Pitfield, Milton Keynes, MK11 3LW, UK
UKHW022007190726
13853UKWH00004B/1795